HALF HUMAN

PANDORA BOX OF HUMAN PSYCHE

THEVA KIRUBA

Glory to God

Contents

Contents

Disclimer

This is a work of fiction. Any names or characters, businesses or places, events or incidents, are fictitious. Any resemblance to actual persons, living or dead, or actual events is purely coincidental.

About The Author

Theva Kiruba is an Indian Poetess, Podcaster and an Aspiring individual with high creative Intelligence who carving for her in depth thought to splash the sparkling colors to the society. Young published author. She holds Bachelor degree in English, Bachelors in education and pursuing her Master's in Holy Cross College, Trichy, India. She is really dynamic about spending her time in writing. She has developed strong sense of writing poetry. She has published more than 60 poems , as well as a book titled

"A Quill with Nectar Drop". She has received

"InkQuill holder award" for her excellence in writing field.

You can listen to her podcast on the following platforms under the name **THEVA PODCAST**

i. **Apple Podcast**

v. **Breaker**

v. **Spotify**

v. **Castbox**

v. **Google podcast**

v. **Radio Public**

v. **TuneIn**

Acknowledgements

Acknowledgement

"The Lord your God will set you high above all the nations on earth. All these blessings will come on you and accompany you if you obey the Lord your God." (Deuteronomy28:1)

Thank you god for your abundant blessings and made this book possible. His name has to be praised in the hallway. He is faithful when I'm faithless. He has done great things in my life. He has raised me from the dust and molded me as an aesthetic colorful Pot.

I extend my sincere gratitude to Dr.Sr. Christina Brigit, Principal of Holy Cross college, Dr. Catherin Edward, Dr.Sr. Judy Gomez, Dr.K.Suganthi, Dr. Cheryl Antonette Dumenil, Ms.Maria Camilla, Mrs.Eileen Brisha and all my English department staff members, Holy Cross college, Trichy, India, for their constant support and motivation

Heartfelt thanks to my parents, Preceleya, Mrs. Devi Shree, Persis Cynthia, friends, all my brothers and sisters, family members for their love and support.

My special thanks to my publishing house and the team, who helped to achieve my dream.

Preface

Preface

Half Human is not a word. It reflects in depth thoughts of human emotions, which deeply rooted to its Past, Present and Future. Entire book trying to knitted up two half of human soul. One half wandering all over the world and another one hide behind the mask. This book is dealing with hiding half, which tries to splash its longingness, desires and stream of consciousness to the world.

Readers be careful! Hiding half may try to escape from this book. Keep it safe!

Happy Journey!

Preface

1. Half Human TOWARDS STRANGE!

I was standing in the middle of trees;
Roses were bloomed everywhere;
Bees were wandering here and there;
Fountain was captured center of attraction to this place;
Edward II was fond of this fountain;
How could I tell him?
Remembrance of his fondness, still exist!
My heart melted towards Swan's Curve;
I could see that couple swan still exchanging their love;
It spread fragrance everywhere;
Fountain's Holy water blessed me twice;
Birds were singing praises;
Stranger was standing next to me;
I asked him, "Where I'm"?
He replied, Garden of Eden!

2. Edges !

It was a beautiful morning;
I was sitting under the tree in old brown bench;
Trees were giggling with each other,
And shedding their leaves;
Wind playing along with those leaves;
Sun was hiding behind the trees;
Even it hide,
Its splashing glitters reached out through the gap of the trees;
Saint's aura behind my head;
It added glitter to my body;
Shadow of mine lean against me;
Dusky light mildly turned to dark;
Birds returned to their branches;
I couldn't move from there,
Coz, Da Vinci stroked me inside the frame!

3. Haunted Flames!

Drowning memories,
Led me into the deep dark;
Tea bags were still floating in the cup;
Clock strike twice for twelve;
I couldn't move;
Still I was there;
Memories haunted me down and down;
No one could understand;
Yes no one!
Longing of my heart,
Burning like flames inside me;
Memories of my identity,
Our identity,
Your identity,
Already trees started to shed leaves from trees;
It swept away to garbage;
Coz of advancement;
We were living in the shades of them;
Shades of olden days;
I was all alone in this room;
Coz everyone busy with their gadgets;
Could you please lend me your ears;

Could you please ?

4. Rainbow crayons!

Wrist watch pins were running fast;
Books pages were dancing towards wind's beat;
Everyone running before me,
But i was still;
Sitting in the chair watching through the window;
There was a huge apple tree;
Flowers were staring to blooming fruits;
A small boy was standing under the tree
With white puppy;
Da Vinci was sitting in the street bench
Beneath the tree and coloring the world;
Puppy running here and there;
It's often disturbing him;
Small boy was trying to catch the puppy;
Both were run over the colors,
It splashed everywhere;
Da Vinci colored the world with rainbow!

5. Bermuda love!

I thought,
we would hiking further more;
But she left me in middle of the sea;
Coz of my fault!
I lost her;
I could see her shadow;
But, I couldn't see her entire face;
Even that too blur for me!
On the way of my sailing,
I could see her in top of the rock;
Between the waves;
Through gentle wind;
But nothing I could figure it out!
I could hear her voice;
Seeking help;
Nothing I could see my naked eyes;
I saw a mermaid blowing flutes from long;
Outreach to shore,
I was asking to myself;
Whether it's my illusion?
Already i was in the middle of the sea;
How could I figured the shore from here;
Fairy warning me again;
I cleanse my eyes with sea water;

And saw that again;
Siren was waiting for me,
in the middle of Bermuda triangle;
Siren!
Sound of siren echoing everywhere;
I tried hard to turned my ship back;
She pulled me hard as I did to escape from there;
She was my competitor now;
I tried hard to push me out;
She did same to pull me inside;
She was begging me;
She was crying;
She mourning that she had no one;
And longing for love;
And was living all alone,
In betwixt the Bermuda Triangle;
Fairy warning me again!
Already I was nearer to it;
I didn't know where to turn,
Finally I fainted!

6. Breezy Silver!

Breezy Silver!

I was laying on the green pastures in the top of the mountain,
Andcounting the stars;
Each stars giggling with each other's and
Playing hide and seek;
Cool breeze smoothen my skin;
Moon applied glitters to my cheeks;
Moon splashing it's light all over the country,
My cycle was my only companion there;
I was conversing with moon for all night;
I felt liter;
I could feel that moon coming closer to me;
He sat next to me;
He put his hand on my shoulder,
I lean on his shoulder;
We both were watching,
Millions of comets,
Chasing each other!

7. Collided assumption!

Small White kitten was under the blanket;
It was so afraid of others;
Green people were showing sympathy;
Blue people were fed her with milk;
Purple people were staring at her;
Grey people were taking snaps with her;
Yellow people felt bad for her;
Orange people were busy with mundane world;
Red people were trying to remove blanket from her;
Brown people were trying to chuck her out;
No one, wouldn't ask her
Why she was afraid?
Why she couldn't come out from blanket ?
Why she looked pale?
No one would know
Coz, no one would ask her;
Every color understood by their own assumption;
Readers! At least you?

8. Rectangle muddy cake!

She dressed half;
Her vein hardly visible to my naked eyes;
Her hair was steel as electric wire;
She looked like brown;
She was five years old with five years experience;
Big mammoth was her god;
Every day she was her in her knees;
Plead for mercy;
But he was foreign to mercy;
Her eyes were longing for something;
But she was betwixt rectangle cakes;
Every day she dumped her desires;
Mrs. Tutor's everyday lesson was her dream;
Always she stared about their blue skirt and white shirt;
But she dressed pantone;
They were playing with their friends in evening;
Every time she was playing with rectangle cake;
Finally, her desires ended with muddy rectangle cakes!

9. No mercy! No Human!

She was howling with the hell of pain;
They were cut off her in vein;
She was yelling with scorn;
Her baby was happen to born;
Could you please stop it for while?
For a while!
Her baby already died,
Before it could reach humankind;
She was yelling,
We were dying in a short
Because of your gunshot;
You were the savage;
Your mind were full of drainage;
One day we would meet in heaven;
You would have to meet my baby fawn;
He would assign a judgment for you;
Hey nasty hunters,
Could you please stop it for while?

10. No peace! I moved on!

I was flying from high to low;
I could see people gossiping about one and another;
There was no peace!
So I moved on!
I was sitting in the top of the tea shop;
I could hear the political criticism;
There was no peace!
So I moved on!
I was sitting near to the market;
Every seller were hold huge baggage of mourning
There was no peace!
So I moved on!
I was sitting near to the window church;
I shocked and frightened about petition bags,
There was no peace!
So I moved on!
I was roaming everywhere,
But, I couldn't find peace nowhere;
There was no peace!
So I moved on!
Finally, I saw a small child playing with butterfly;
I wished to play with her;
Her smile melted my heart;
I found peace, so I stayed!

11. Black soldiers!

I used to blindly following my friend;
We were crew of black soldiers;
We had to work for twenty four;
We hardly fought for our food;
Winter was our enemy;
We used to carry our food on our shoulder;
We were punctual;
We designed to be disciplined;
We used to follow one and another;
Our march might not visible to human world;
Because we were too small;
There was no recognition in the human world;
But we were not tired of anything;
We would follow our destination;
We would live in our own tiny world!

12. Unwritten stories!

I was sitting in the window seat of the bus;
And peeping through the window;
I could see number and number of heads;
Each one's eyes would tell different stories;
Stories of waiting;
Stories of longing;
Stories of searching;
I saw a small girl selling beats;
She came to me,
Asked which you want?
But I asked her, whether she was going school?
Her eyes were rolled in tears;
And she ran to her mom;
I could understand the pain,
And longing of her small heart;
I felt ashamed about our society;
I too couldn't do anything for her;
Felt ashamed!

13. Happy Echoes!

I was walking in the long road;
And it was most beautiful one,
That I'd ever seen in my life;
The road was fully covered with green;
It's like sheet of green pastures,
Carrying the long;
The road covered with deep silence;
But I could hear echoes of my heartbeat everywhere;
Yes, purest form of echoes;
True longing of peace;
They're happy echoes,
Coz, it reached the destination;
Roads were the barriers of trees;
Trees were filled with birds;
Its chirping voice echoing along with my heartbeat;
I could hear the conversations of honey bees in the hive;
Actually they were celebrating the party in the hive;
No drama!
No pain!
Only sound of peace I could hear here!

14. Scares were beautiful!

My heart was binded by bandages;
Scares were stitched by patches of clothes;
I couldn't remove the pins;
Which was shot by closed ones;
I never expected this much of pins;
But , scares were beautiful;
Even it was painful,
But I loved the scare;
They were love wounds;
My friends and relatives,
Gave me this gift;
When everyone left me
All alone only with scares;
Still my scares were shine
And it took beautiful!

15. Truest longing!

I was lying on the green pasture
And looking the sky;
I could see the heaven;
God was very busy in creating new human from dust;
And sometimes he happened to hear some
Request and partition and to solve the problem;
He also too busy to hear my voice;
In this planet no one was there to hear my voice;
Everyone was busy with their own work;
Everyone had their own problems;
No one could,
Yup, no one was there to quench my soul's thirst;
My truest longing only for a person to hear the voice of my soul;
I need a person to quench the thirsty of my soul;
My soul was longing for something,
Which I couldn't early explain!

16. A Garden next to Eden!

There was a beautiful garden;
No one entered it before it;
I was the one who entered first;
I'd never seen such an aesthetic garden;
With heavenly flowers and trees;
I could feel peacefulness everywhere;
It was an early morning;
New dawning of the day,
with chill breeze ;
Really I felt heavenly calmness,
Which I wanted the most in my life;
I could see droplets of snow,
In each tips of the leaves;
Green pastures were more green in color;
Sky was looking cool;
Such a lovely nature;
Creator's hand, made wonder;
His best ever masterpiece!

17. Until it off!

I was playing piano in the middle of woods;
Flames of fire were burning around me in a circle;
Monster and giants were waiting out for me,
Till it off;
Sounds from the keys were more horrible;
That splashing fears of water to my soul more and more;
Echoes of the music bouncing between the woods;
They were fiercer than I expect;
Their howling sound felt like tightened of muscles;
Already it pierced my friend into pieces;
Who would save me;
My soul was yelling loud in the torment of pain;
Flames were slowly growing down;
They were eagerly waiting;
My lungs were pumping with heavy pressure;
Entire fire went down;
They were entered,
I become unconscious;
Form distance I could see the light;
That reached to me;
It took me in its hands;
At last, I was sleeping peacefully in its hand!

18. Could I feel little more!

Could I feel little more!

Roses were surrounded everywhere
Wind was blowing gently;
It was stealing some petals from the roses;
And decorated Emma's wedding dress;
Her entire wedding dress fully covered with happiness;
She was twinkling like a star with extreme emotions;
That she could feel like,
Rats were running inside her tummy;
That's she could explain out;
She was overwhelmed with joy;
Meanwhile she couldn't handle her fear;
Her mother could read everything,
By looking Emma's eyes;
She hugged Emma tightly,
And said we were going to miss her;
Both eyes rolled with tears,
And stepping towards her wedding!

19. Because of them!

All those memories were hunting me every day!
Grudges, howling, deep dark everywhere;
Couldn't take further step;
I stuck in a room for all day and night;
Those empty cups of tea cups drained like me;
My eyes had no more tears,
Yes it's gone!
I could feel that was in the empty room,
Even it filled with everything;
Flowers could feel for me,
Rather them;
Flowers were started losing their petals for me;
Even they were also in grief;
Birds were shedding tears for me;
Deeper clouds were growing,
They too blast out their thunders and lightening for me;
Entire world grew dark for me;
There was no light;
Still I had a hope,
One day we would join together!

20. Archived snaps!

We used to walk in beach;
Breezy wind!
Sound of waves!
Our smiles would be my most beautiful memories!
We were three,
We always spend our days together;
We danced together;
We dreamt together;
And we worked together;
Everyone wondered about our friendship;
We would be the highlighted crew in the parties;
We would exchange our clothes too!
But now everything became a memory;
They were not going to be in my life anymore;
They were living with me in memories;
Beautiful memories but in snaps!

21. Quotes!

Invoking twist blasting thoughts in lines...

22. Quote 1

"Good memories consoles your soul, while
Bad Memories sucks your soul as vampire drained blood!"

23. Quote 2

"Always accept!

Never expect!"

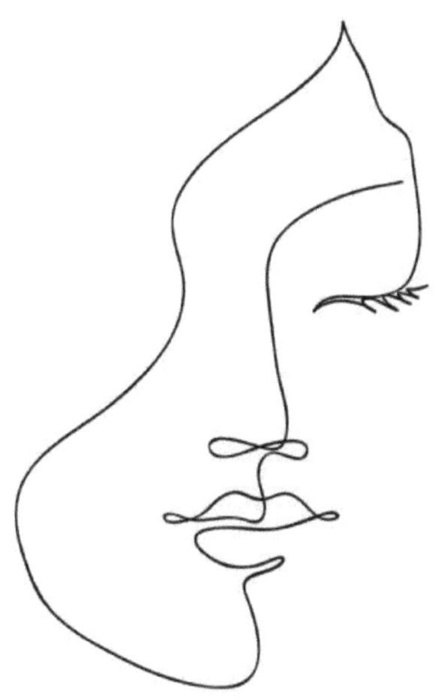

24. Quote 3

"If life rejects you from one thing,

don't think it's a rejection

actually it protect you from danger and lead you

towards most biggest thing , which deserves you the most!"

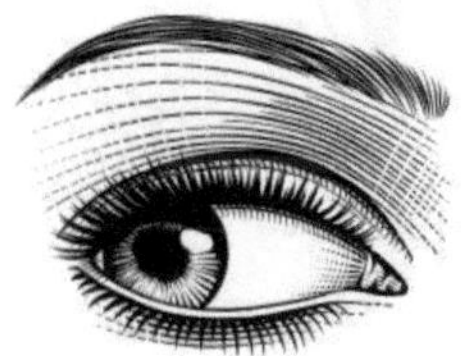
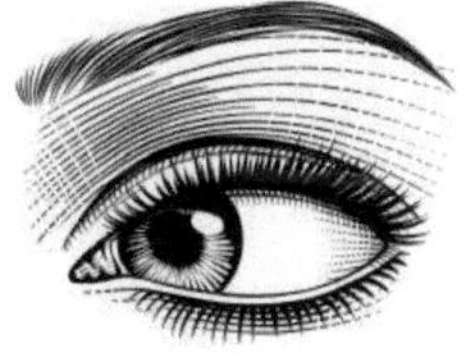

25. Quote 4

" Everything is just an decorative illusion!"

26. Quote 5

"Stay single until you find your loyal soul companion!"

27. Quote 6

"If someone avoiding you,

Bless them to be enjoy their life without you!"

28. Quote 7

" Be quite but secretly observe everything!"

29. Quote 8

"Nobody really cares you,

Take care of yourself!"

30. Quote 9

"Enjoy every moment of life, rather expecting that from others!"

31. Quote 10

"Stay, where your soul feel like home!"

32. Quote 11

"Life will not bless you twice with same treasure, wake up!"

THE END

Printed by Libri Plureos GmbH in Hamburg,
Germany